PRECIOUS MOMENTS™

What A Wonderful World

A GOLDEN BOOK • NEW YORK

Western Publishing Company, Inc., Racine, Wisconsin 53404

God gave this world to you and me.

It's priceless, yet it's also free.

It's beautiful beyond compare,

and He has left it in our care.

Every day begins anew,

like a rose sparkling with the dew.

They blossom in the morning sun

and bloom until the day is done.

A little seed becomes a tree

and gives its shade to you and me.

Every creature,
great and small,

the Lord above has made them all.

The bear, the bee, the kangaroo

all share this world with me and you.

High above us in the sky,

we watch the silver
clouds go by.

They bring the gentle rain our way,

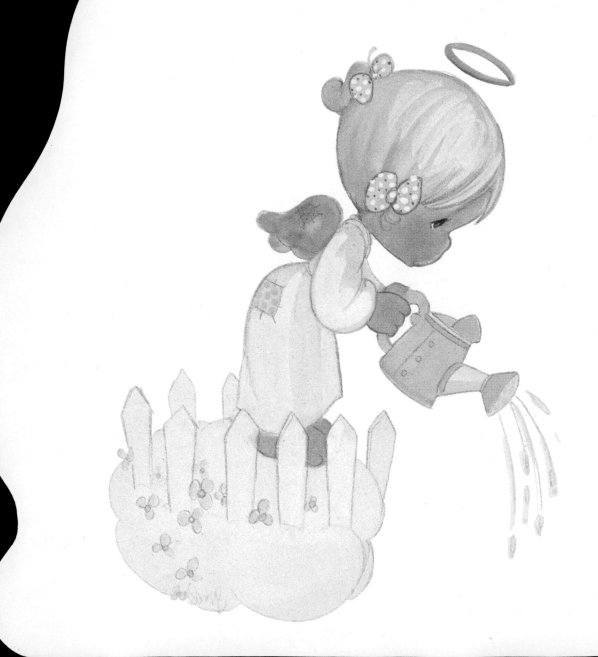

and rainbows brighten

up our day.

And as we watch the setting sun,

another perfect day is done.

G od gave this world to you and me.

He lit the stars above.

By seeing all the things He made . . .

we know that God is love.